A STEVEN SPIELBERG PRESENTATION
AN AMERICAN TAIL ™
THE ILLUSTRATED STORY

Adapted by EMILY PERL KINGSLEY
From a screenplay by JUDY FREUDBERG & TONY GEISS
Based upon characters created by DAVID KIRSCHNER

Illustrated by
DAVID KIRSCHNER
BEVERLY LAZOR-BAHR
CHRISTINE FINN

Designed by DEBORAH BETHEL

PlayValue Books®
A Division of Grosset & Dunlap

Prologue
AMERICA 1986

"But I've told it to you a hundred times . . . a thousand times." The wizened old mouse, whose fur had turned to gray many years before and whose whiskers were now as white as snow, patted the head of the great-grandchild who sat on his lap.

"Tell me again, Great-Grandpa Fievel, *please!* Tell me about the old days—when you were little—how there was no radio or TV! Tell me about what it was like when you lived in Russia, and the boat, and the cats, and how you felt when you first came to America! Please, Great-Grandpa Fievel . . . *please!*"

The ancient mouse sighed, settled in against the soft pillows of the deep armchair, and drew the child close to his side.

"Ah, it was such a long time ago . . . so many, many years ago. When I was a boy in Russia we lived in a tiny town. I remember it was Chanukah . . ."

3

Chapter One
RUSSIA 1885

*C*hanukah! A festival of light and joy! And in the tiny home of the Mousekewitz family, the celebration went on long into the night. The Mousekewitzes lived in a small village in Russia. Like most of the other mice in their village they were quite poor. This family, however, was filled with love and warmth, and was very content with the simple life they led. Being together as a family was always the most important thing to them. Although they were poor, Mama and Papa always managed to make the holidays seem very special to the children.

As the sun went down, little Fievel and Tanya lit the candles in the menorah and recited the ancient prayers. Fievel was seven years old, and his sister Tanya was eight. The children both loved the holidays. They looked forward to Chanukah all year long. After they said their prayers the family settled down for a huge dinner—bread crumbs, bread-crumb stuffing, and bread-crumb pudding for dessert.

Later, when the special holiday dishes had been washed and put away, Papa Mousekewitz played lively tunes on the violin. Papa was the kind of father that every child dreams of having. He lived for his children's happiness, and at Chanukah it was especially evident. Fievel and Tanya danced and danced to Papa's violin until the room was spinning around them.

Mama Mousekewitz rocked baby Yasha in her lap and tapped her foot in time with the music. For Mama as well, her family was her life. Raising the three children and providing a home for them and for Papa filled her days with the

simple joys of living. This year she had outdone herself with her magnificent holiday feast.

Fievel ran to Papa, gave him a big hug, and said, "Papa, play the song you wrote for me. My special song."

Papa smiled and looked at his little boy. Fievel loved the song that Papa had composed just for him, and it gave Papa a thrill to watch as Tanya and Fievel whirled around the little room hand in hand, while Papa played it.

"Is it time for our presents?" asked Tanya, when the music was over and the room had stopped lurching.

"Ahhhh . . . your presents! What is Chanukah without presents?" said Papa, beaming. He pulled a rolled-up scarf from behind his back and presented it to Tanya. The scarf was quite old and worn and had been patched and repaired many times, but Tanya's eyes glowed with happiness.

"A new babushka!" she exclaimed. "Oh, it's beautiful! Thank you, Papa."

"You have only one parent?" asked Mama.

"Thank you, Mama," said Tanya, giving her mother a big hug.

"And for my big son, Fievel," Papa went on, "something very special . . ."

Papa reached up, took off his hat, and placed it on Fievel's head.

"Your hat," whispered Fievel, in awe. "Your own hat."

"Not just *my* hat," said Papa with pride, "but my *father's* hat, and *his* father's before him. This hat has been in our family for three generations. And now it is yours!"

Fievel ran to look at himself in the mirror. The hat was much too big and fell over his eyes, but he felt very proud and very important.

"Don't worry, my boy," said Papa, "you will soon grow into it. Wear it proudly." Papa thought of the day he received the hat from his father, and a small tear of joy, mixed with remembrance, came to his eye.

"Oh, I will wear it proudly," whispered Fievel. "Thank you, Papa. Thank you, Mama."

"And now, a Chanukah story!" said Papa, looking at his children and feeling like a rich man, despite his poverty.

Tanya and Fievel climbed into their father's lap. Tanya wanted the story about the mouse with the long hair that the prince climbed up. Fievel wanted the story about the mouse who pricked her finger and fell asleep for a hundred years. But Papa told them a new story—a story about the Giant Mouse of Minsk.

"The Giant Mouse of Minsk," Papa explained, "was as tall as a tree! His tail was a mile long! He was so big he frightened all the cats!"

"Shhh!" interrupted Mama. "Not so loud! Don't talk about cats. Tell them about something else! It's Chanukah!"

Tanya jumped up. "America! Tell us about America, Papa!"

"America? You want to hear about *America*? Let me see . . . in America, there are mouseholes in every wall!"

Fievel's eyes widened with amazement. "Really?"

"Fairy tales," said Mama.

"Really," Papa went on. "There are bread crumbs on every floor! In America you can say anything you want. And in America," Papa took a deep breath and continued, "there are no . . . *cats!*"

"Quiet," whispered Mama. "They'll hear you!"

"How could they hear us?" asked Papa.

Suddenly, the house began to jump and shake. The sound of horses' hooves clattering through the town and the shouts of terrified people made all the mice tremble with fear.

"The Cossacks! The Cossacks!"

In those days, from time to time, Cossacks would gallop through the Jewish villages of Russia, burning homes and temples, destroying everything in their path. In the same kind of way, *cat*-Cossacks, known as *Catsacks*, would race through the tiny Russian *mouse* villages, burning and demolishing the little mouse homes and capturing whole mouse families as they ran from their flaming houses out into the snow.

This particular Chanukah night was an especially dreadful attack. The Cat-sacks were throwing blazing torches into every corner and chasing mice with their fearsome claws and blood-curdling yowls.

By the next morning, the entire mouse village was a charred and smoking ruin. The Mousekewitz family felt fortunate to be alive. They stood together in silence, looking at the blackened remains of their world. At their feet lay the few possessions they had been able to drag from the flames before their home was completely destroyed.

"In America," whispered Papa, fighting back the tears, "in America there are no cats!"

"America," said Fievel, turning over the sound in his mouth. It sounded good. "America."

Chapter Two
THE VOYAGE

In the 1880s thousands of mice from all over Europe who had experienced the hardship of poverty and the terror of the continuing vicious attacks by marauding cats left their homes and began the long, difficult journey to find a new and better world in America. Mice came from Russia, from Poland, from Greece, Italy, Romania, Ireland, Germany, France, Hungary, and Czechoslovakia.

After many, many months of trudging through fields and along dusty roads, Papa Mousekewitz and his family found themselves at a dock in the great city of Hamburg, in Germany. Looming far above them was the enormous ship that was leaving the next day for America. Gathering up their meager belongings, they inched up the mooring rope "gangplank" and boarded the ship.

Fievel was terribly excited and full of questions as he climbed up the precariously swinging rope. "Look, Papa, is that the ocean? Are those birds seagulls? What is that smoke coming out of the boat?" With each question Fievel stopped, and all the mice behind him almost fell off the rope.

"Keep walking!" they yelled.

"Fievel," said Papa. "This is the last time I take you to America!"

Finally, after what seemed like an endless wait to Fievel, the great whistle blew. The ship, loaded to bursting with people and mice all seeking a new beginning in America, left the pier and steamed out into the great Atlantic Ocean.

Down in the deepest darkest corner of the hold, the Mousekewitz family huddled together. Papa played Fievel's special tune on the violin they had saved from the fire, and the sweet, familiar music made them feel just slightly less afraid of the great adventure ahead. Tanya peered through the darkness at the hundreds of families, all starting out on this momentous journey.

"I'm afraid," whispered Tanya. "Maybe we should have stayed in Russia."

"Don't worry," reassured Papa. "As long as we're together, we'll be all right."

Little Fievel wasn't worried. He was too excited to be worried. Every day was filled with new experiences, new sensations, new sights and smells and feelings. He explored every inch of the cabin in which the mice families lay clinging to each other and, in fact, sometimes ventured out into the larger part of the ship where the human passengers milled about.

It was there that Fievel discovered the three gigantic herring barrels. Papa, worried about where his son had wandered off to this time, finally found Fievel staring with fascination into a barrel full of pickled herring.

"What are they, Papa?" asked Fievel excitedly.

"They are herring, my son. A kind of fish," said Papa. Papa explained to his curious son that these fish in the barrel were dead—pickled for people to eat. "But," Papa went on, "the sea out there is full of fish, live fish, herring and many other kinds of fish."

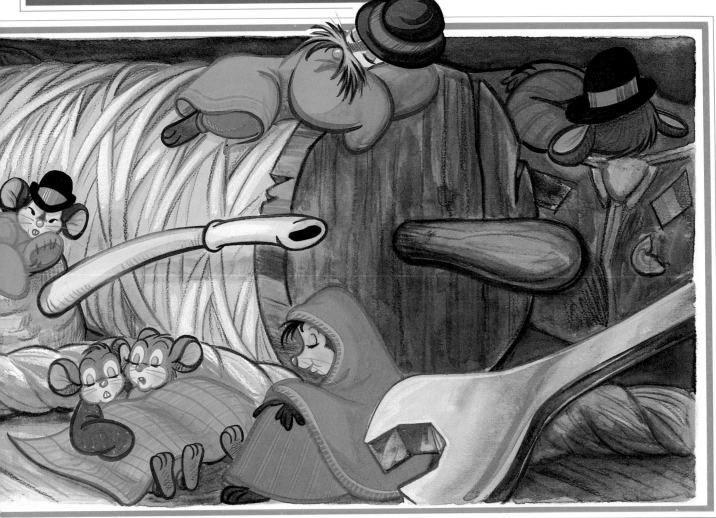

"Can we go see them, Papa?" asked Fievel.

Papa didn't answer. He simply dragged Fievel back to the protected corner where Mama, Tanya, and Yasha were waiting for them.

"Where did you find him this time?" asked Mama.

"Getting acquainted with some fish," answered Papa.

The voyage dragged on. Each day blended into the next, and the weeks rolled by. One day, in the middle of the ocean, the ship encountered a terrible storm. Thunder crashed and driving rain pelted the ship with a fury. Heavy as it was, with its bulging cargo of people and mice bound for America, the ship was tossed about on the huge waves like a tiny cork. Inside the vessel, mice and people alike were horribly seasick from the awful rolling and lurching.

Mama Mousekewitz looked around but didn't see her son. "Where is Fievel?" she asked. "Where is that boy now?"

Fievel was off again, riding on a slippery cake of soap that slid back and forth through the cabin as the ship pitched and rocked in the storm.

"Fievel! Come back! Sit here with us!" called Mama. "Oh, that boy!"

"I'll go get him," offered Papa, and he staggered off in the direction of the zooming bar of soap, trying to keep his feet on the rocking boat.

"Wheee!" Fievel shrieked, as his soap slid crazily from one side of the ship to the other.

With a thump, Fievel's soap crashed into the bottom of a staircase, and he tumbled off. The staircase led directly up onto the deck of the ship. As Fievel stared up the stairs with fascination, a huge wave crashed onto the deck and several flip-flopping fish came cascading down the stairs. Fievel was amazed, and scampered up the steps to see more. Just as Papa arrived at the bottom of the stairs, Fievel reached the top and poked his head out the door to look at the outer deck. The deck seemed alive with fish that had been washed aboard by the tumultuous waves, fish everywhere, flapping wildly up and down.

"Fievel!" shouted Papa, in a panic. "Fievel, come back! Get down from there!"

"Fish, Papa!" yelled Fievel. "Look at all the fish!"

Seasick as he was, Papa raced up the stairs and tried to grab Fievel's hand to pull him back downstairs, but Fievel had already run out onto the deck to see the fish. Before his horrified eyes, Papa watched as Fievel was picked up by a giant wave and tossed back and forth. "*No!*" shouted Papa.

"Help! Papa!" screamed Fievel. "Help me!"

"Fievel! Take my hand, grab my hand!" Papa reached and reached, but the wave swept across the ship and carried little Fievel overboard.

"Fievel!" shouted Papa, as his heart shattered into a million pieces. "My boy . . . my baby," he whimpered. Then he broke down and cried uncontrollably.

The ship continued to chug away, unaware and unconcerned that one little mouse was floundering in the ocean, farther and farther behind in its wake, calling, "Papa . . . Papa . . ."

Chapter Three
ARRIVALS

Many days later, when the ship finally docked in New York Harbor, the Mousekewitz family joined the throng of mice from all over the world who lined up under the IMMIGRATION sign to be admitted to America. Mice from every corner of the world chattered in dozens of different languages as they huddled together in little family groupings. Clutching their tiny bundles of belongings, the only reminders of the lives they had left behind, they looked around with apprehension, wondering what lay ahead for each little family in this great new land.

Once inside the enormous Immigration Hall, the mice were subjected to various examinations, such as mental and physical tests, to see if they were healthy and fit to enter America.

When the Mousekewitzes finally found themselves before the Registration Desk, the Immigration officer asked Papa Mousekewitz their names and how many in their family. Once again the horror of that day came rushing back to Papa, with thoughts of his poor lost Fievel, swept overboard into the tumbling sea. Papa wiped a tear and murmured, "We are only four . . . now."

The officer stamped the papers and passed the four remaining Mousekewitzes through the door—into America.

Meanwhile, only a few hundred yards away, an old bottle floated in on the tide and washed up on the shore of Bedloe's Island in New York Harbor. As soon as the bottle stopped bobbing, out popped a little head wearing a hat that was just a little bit too big for it. It was Fievel Mousekewitz, a little waterlogged, but alive!

"Welcome to America, my little immigrant," said a pigeon with a heavy French accent. The pigeon helped Fievel out of his bottle and tried to dry him off.

Fievel looked around the island. "America?" he asked, puzzled. "I thought it was bigger."

"It is," said Henri, pointing at the mainland. "All that is also America!"

"Are you an American?" asked Fievel.

"Oh, no, no, *mon ami,*" replied the pigeon. "I am Henri le Pigeon, from France. I am here to put up my statue. Liberty is her name. Is she not lovely? Ah, well, she *will* be when we have her all together. And what about you, little one? Where is your family? You are quite young to be traveling all by yourself."

Fievel told the pigeon all about his family coming to America on the boat, how he was washed overboard by a wave, and how he had clung to the bottle all the way to shore.

"I am afraid I will never see my family again," sobbed Fievel. "America is such a big place and I wouldn't know where to begin to look for them!"

"Now, now. You are too young to give up hope," started Henri. "Pick your chin up, my little friend. In America, there is always hope. You must *never* say never. Begin at Immigration," he suggested. "*Everybody* enters America through Immigration. My friend Chantal will fly you over to the Immigration Building where I am sure you will find your Mama and Papa. I would take you myself but I cannot leave my statue."

Fievel became hopeful. He thanked Henri, climbed onto the back of the other pigeon, and waved good-bye.

"You must come back and see my beautiful statue when she is all finished," called Henri. "I will come and get you! Good luck, my little friend!"

Chantal the pigeon soared into the air with the little mouse aboard, and wheeled off in the direction of the great Immigration Hall.

Chapter Four
A FRIEND?

Once outside the Immigration Hall, Papa Mousekewitz took a deep breath and looked around. America. They were in America at last. He was still deeply sorrowful at the loss of his beloved little Fievel, but he tried to pull himself together, gather what was left of his little family, and start off to find a place for them to live.

A moment later, Fievel's pigeon escort flipped him off her back and the little mouse fell to the ground right at the spot his family had just left. He picked himself up and looked anxiously through the crowds of mouse families entering the new land and starting their new lives. Nowhere could he see his Papa, Mama, his sister Tanya, or Yasha, the baby—hundreds and hundreds of mouse families,

but not a sign of *his.*

Suddenly, a large rat appeared beside Fievel and offered his hand.

"Rat's the name," said the rat. "Warren T. Rat. You appear to be in some sort of difficulty. How may I help you?"

"I'm trying to find my family," said Fievel, still craning his neck, standing on tiptoes as he tried to spot his missing loved ones.

"I can help you find them," murmured the rat smoothly. "I know exactly where they are. Just come along with me."

"But my friend the pigeon said they'd be right here, at Immigration."

"Would I mislead you, kid? I'll take you right to them. Trust me." Warren T. Rat took little Fievel by the hand and led him off.

Before long, Fievel and Warren T. Rat arrived at bustling Hester Street in New York City. Thousands of mice who had just arrived in America seemed to settle on this busy street. Fievel was fascinated with the teeming activity—

pushcarts and mice everywhere, the smell of cooking foods of every possible nationality, the babble of dozens of different languages as mothers called to their children and hawkers sold their wares.

"Come along, my boy. Come along," urged Warren T. Rat, dragging little Fievel along the crowded sidewalk. "You'll never find your family if you poke along like that."

"It's all so amazing," breathed Fievel. "I've never seen anything like it!"

In a back room, way upstairs in a tenement Fievel had just walked past with Warren T. Rat, the little Mousekewitz family tried to resume some sort of normal life without Fievel. Mama sewed a large pile of shirts. Tanya watched quietly as Papa lit a memorial candle under Fievel's picture.

"I have this feeling that Fievel is still alive somewhere," said Tanya.

"It will go away," said Mama sadly. "In time it will go away."

Papa looked at her, picked up his violin, and began to play a slow, mournful tune. A dull mournfulness filled his soul, but he played on, keeping Fievel's spirit alive.

Fievel, very much alive, was at that moment being ushered into a room unlike any he'd ever seen before. Over the door was a sign that read MOE'S SWEATSHOP.

"What's a sweatshop?" asked Fievel, excitedly.

"You'll see, you'll see," Warren T. Rat said, grinning.

The room was poorly lit by a single kerosene lantern, but Fievel could see dozens and dozens of mice hard at work making hundreds of little mouse shirts, pants, and dresses. Some of the mice cut out the garments with great big shears. Others huddled over rows of sewing machines that clattered and squeaked. Still others bent over ironing boards, pressing the little garments with hot flat-

irons. The air was heavy and steamy, and some of the mice coughed deeply as they worked.

Warren T. Rat spoke hurriedly with Moe, the rat in charge, who gulped and handed over a thick wad of dollar bills.

"Seventeen dollars! That's an awful lot of money," Moe complained.

"Isn't it worth seventeen bucks to keep the cats away, Moe old pal? Y'don't see any cats around here, do you? Let's keep it that way, okay?"

Moe nodded miserably as Warren T. Rat brought Fievel over to his desk.

"I brought you a new worker, Moe. Don't thank me. Just send me his salary!"

Fievel had been looking around the busy room, standing on tiptoes. "I don't see my family in here, Mr. Rat," he said, turning to leave.

"You don't need a family anymore, kid," laughed Warren T. Rat. "You've got yourself a job!" And he left the crowded sweatshop, chuckling to himself.

"But I thought—" started Fievel.

"We don't pay you to think!" yelled Moe, who dumped a huge pile of cloth into Fievel's arms and pushed him toward the mice who were bent over the sewing machines. "Get to work! Get back to work *everybody!*"

Chapter Five
A REAL FRIEND

As Fievel joined the army of mice working day and night in Moe's Sweatshop, he came to realize that they were all captives in the steamy room, and none of the mice held any hope of ever getting out!

One day, carrying a huge pile of garments, Fievel collided with another mouse who carried a similar pile in his arms. The little suits, shirts, and jackets flew all over the place. Fievel and the other mouse dug their way out of the mound of garments. The new mouse was an immigrant from Italy and he and Fievel shook hands. His name was Tony Toponi. Tony was older than Fievel. He was an orphan who had been living on his own for many years. He was a streetwise mouse who knew all the angles.

"I'm Tony. Tony Toponi. You're new here, aren't you?" he began.

"Yes," replied Fievel. "I'm Fievel . . . Fievel Mousekewitz. I just arrived from Russia."

"Well, you're in America now," said Tony. "You ought to have a more American-sounding name. Suppose we call you . . . Phil! Philly! That's it, we'll call you Philly!"

Fievel shrugged. America was full of strange things: getting locked in a room full of workers who never were allowed to leave, receiving a new name from a stranger who just met you. It was more than he could easily understand. But, he figured, this was America, so you do things the American way.

"You here in America all by yourself, Philly?" asked Tony.

"No," said Fievel. "I came with my family, but we got separated. I have to get out of here so I can find them!"

Although Tony was streetwise, he had a big heart. He immediately took a liking to little Fievel, and felt protective of his new friend.

Several other mice working nearby laughed at Fievel's talk of getting out.

"You'll never get out of here!" said one.

"Nobody's ever gotten out of here!" added another sadly.

"Only way out of here is out the window! And it's ten stories straight down!" said a third.

"I wish we had that mouse from the fairy tale," said Fievel, looking down at the street, "the one with the long, long hair. Then we could climb down."

The mice laughed at the ridiculous idea, but suddenly stopped laughing. Perhaps the idea was *not* so ridiculous. Tony Toponi whispered a fantastic suggestion to one of the mice sitting next to him. That mouse passed the idea on to the next mouse. Before long the whole room was buzzing with excited whispers.

"*Back to work!*" screamed Moe.

The mice turned back to their work with new purpose, cutting and sewing with energy and enthusiasm. Fievel and Tony kept a steady stream of cloth coming to the workers who cut and stitched feverishly.

Several days later, they were ready. At a signal from Tony, three mice crept up behind Moe the rat and quickly tied him to his chair. Three other mice carried a huge pile of suits to the open window. Tying one end to a radiator, they pushed the ball of material out the window and it unrolled and unrolled and became a long rope of suits and shirts, all sewn together into a ladder of clothing that reached all the way down to the street below.

One by one the gleeful mice climbed down the ladder of suits and escaped the imprisoning sweatshop. Tony and Fievel were the last to leave and never looked back at the dismal room that had been "home" to so many unfortunate mice.

When they jumped off the ladder and onto the sidewalk, they breathed

deeply the fresh outside air. Fievel shook Tony's hand and explained that now he was going to get back to the business of locating his missing family. Tony put a protective arm around the little mouse's shoulders. He was growing quite fond of Fievel.

"You know," said Tony. "I'm getting along fine without my family, but if you want, I'll help you find yours."

"Oh, would you?" breathed Fievel. "That would be wonderful! I don't know where to start."

Over the next few days their friendship grew. Fievel and Tony searched the neighborhood for Fievel's family. Any time Fievel spotted a mouse wearing Russian-style clothes, he was sure it was his Papa or Mama—but it never was, and Fievel became more and more discouraged.

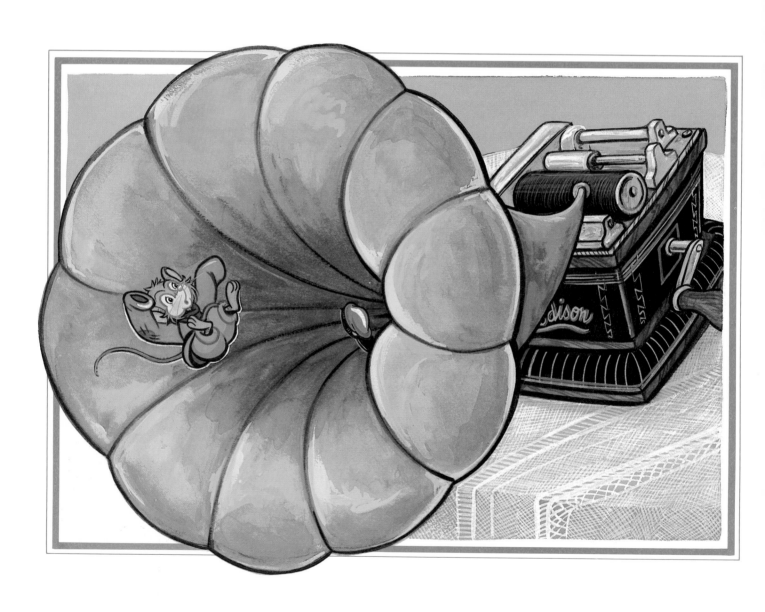

One time, Fievel heard sweet violin music floating down a busy street. He stopped in his tracks and his ears perked up. "Papa?" he cried out, filled with hope. This time he was sure it was Papa playing the violin for his lost son.

Fievel ran across the busy street, scampered up the front of the building, and walked across a high clothesline headed toward the open window from which the music got louder and louder.

Fievel peeked in with great anticipation, only to be disappointed once again. He found himself staring into the belled horn of a large phonograph. The music was not coming from Papa at all, but from a cylindrical record playing on the phonograph.

Fievel sat on the edge of the horn and heaved a heavy sigh. Suddenly his hat slipped off and rolled down the horn. He chased it and soon found himself running in place on the moving musical cylinder. This changed the sound of the music so that people in the apartment took notice.

"It's a mouse!" came the panicked scream from inside the apartment.

Just as Fievel grabbed his hat, a slipper thrown by the frightened human knocked Fievel off the phonograph and out the window. He caught hold of the clothesline and scrambled to the street, exhausted, frazzled, and very unhappy.

One day, as Fievel and Tony continued their search, they turned a corner into an alley and found that a large group of mice had assembled there. Tony stopped in his tracks and stared. At the head of the gathering, standing on a matchbox, was the most beautiful mouse Tony had ever seen.

Her name was Bridget and she had recently arrived in America from Ireland. Her parents had been killed in a cat raid and she was fast becoming a leader of the increasingly outspoken No-Cats Movement. Behind her hung hand-lettered signs and banners reading CATS UNFAIR and MICE UNITE.

As Tony stood and gaped, Bridget addressed the crowd of mice with fiery conviction.

"I'm askin' you now," she cried, her voice lilting with an Irish accent, "are we gonna stand by and let those *cats* wreck our homes?"

The crowd rippled with fear. "Don't say that word," they murmured, trembling. "They'll hear you. They're everywhere!"

Tony pushed his way through the crowd until he stood at Bridget's feet, staring up into her beautiful face, flushed with excitement and determination.

"Don't you understand?" cried Bridget. "This is America! You can say anything you like here! You can say *cat* as much as you want to! Listen: *cat! Cat!! CAT!!!*"

"No, no! Don't say that! They'll hear you!" the crowd protested.

Tony began to chant along with Bridget as the crowd of mice grew more and more upset. "Cat . . . Cat . . . Cat!"

Bridget went on, "And if we all get together, I am sayin' that we could *do* something about the cats!"

Fievel was very confused. He tugged at Tony's sleeve. "I don't understand what everybody's so worried about. Everyone knows there are no cats in America," Fievel said, remembering his Papa's words.

Some of the mice standing next to Fievel looked up, caught their breath, and raced off down the alley as fast as they could.

"There's nothing to be afraid of," Fievel continued. "Why are you running away? What's the matter with you?" he called as more and more mice started scurrying away. "My Papa told me! There are no cats! None!"

But the mice all dashed away and Fievel found himself in the alley with

nothing but the crumpled DOWN WITH CATS signs. Suddenly he heard a terrible sound behind him—a low, growling, snarling sound of enormous menace. Somehow he seemed to remember that sound from Russia, and the Catsacks. Slowly, ever so slowly, he turned around and found himself nose-to-nose with the largest, meanest, ugliest, fiercest cat he'd ever seen.

"Yikes!" screamed Fievel as the cat swiped at him with an enormous paw, its five razor-sharp claws fully extended. By sheer luck, Fievel squirted out of the grasp of the deadly creature, darted out of the alley, and hid under a nearby barrel.

Dozens of cats poured out of the alley on a malicious rampage, smashing and overturning pushcarts, destroying anything they came across and strewing the wreckage everywhere. Mice trembled in fear wherever they could find a corner in which to conceal themselves.

Only when the marauding monsters had demolished everything in sight did they turn and gallop off to terrorize the mice community in the next neighborhood.

After all was quiet, Fievel cautiously poked his head out and looked around at the destruction. Tony and Bridget had hidden themselves in a pair of shoes, and when the cats finally left, they climbed out and found an outraged Fievel standing beside them on the sidewalk.

"My Papa said there were no cats in America!" Fievel said angrily. "Wait till I tell him about *this!*" Then he stopped and added sadly, "If I ever find him."

"What do you mean, if you ever find him?" asked Bridget.

"This is Philly," said Tony, introducing Fievel.

Tony explained to Bridget about Fievel having gotten separated from his family. "I've been trying to help him find them but so far we've had no luck at all," he went on.

"Wait," cried Bridget. "I have an idea! Let's go ask Honest John at Tammany Hall! He knows every mouse in the city! I'm sure he'll be knowin' where to find your family!"

"Oh, Bridget, you're wonderful," cried Fievel.

"Just what I was about to say," breathed Tony, taking Bridget's hand. Bridget blushed to the roots of her bright red fur and murmured, "Come on, let's be goin'."

As the three mice hurried off to find Honest John, other mice were beginning to creep out of their hiding places in the wake of the cats' destruction. Out from under a tin can popped Papa and Mama Mousekewitz.

"So," taunted Mama, "Mister 'There-Are-No-Cats-In-America!' What have you got to say now?"

"Well," started Papa, then he simply shrugged his shoulders and raised his eyes to the heavens.

Chapter Six
A NEW HOPE

Honest John had been in New York for several years and had risen to a position of considerable political power within the immigrant mouse community. He tried to be present at all mouse weddings, christenings, and funerals. In fact, it was at a wake for a young Irish mouse who had died fighting the cats that Tony, Bridget, and Fievel finally found him.

Dressed in a fine cutaway suit, sporting a shiny black top hat, he glanced at his large gold watch as he patted the hand of the young widow.

"What a terrible day," he intoned. "This is my third wake today and I'm not finished yet."

"Those terrible cats!" said a police mouse standing next to Honest John. "Something must be done!"

"We pay Warren T. Rat for protection from the cats, but the attacks keep coming. We get no protection at all!" complained another young mouse.

"Precisely why I am here!" came a voice from the doorway. All conversation stopped and all heads turned toward the voice.

Standing in the door of the modest mouse apartment was the famous Gussie Mausheimer, the richest and most powerful mouse in New York. Gussie had come to New York from Germany some years before and had become immensely rich and influential. A public-spirited mouse, she was well-known for having contributed large amounts of money to many mouse charities, museums, libraries, hospitals, and parks.

"Good to see you, Gussie," said Honest John, oozing charm as he bowed

and kissed her gloved hand. "What brings you down to this part of the city?"

"I am absolutely fed up with these terrible cats! The destruction they have brought upon rich and poor alike is simply dreadful!" Gussie sniffed and dabbed her eye with an elegant lace handkerchief.

Honest John shook his head. "Yes, yes, of course we all agree, Gussie. But what can anybody do?"

"Do? I just know we can come up with a reasonable course of action if we all get together!" said Gussie. "That is why I feel we must have a rally! Tomorrow come to Mausheimer Park. Everybody. I'll bring the uptown mice. You bring the mice from downtown."

Gussie went to the poor widow of the little mouse who had been killed by the cats. "Here," she said, handing the bereaved wife some money from her dainty velvet purse. "Use this to buy a coffin so you can bury him. Don't thank me. I love to help." And she gathered her elegant fur cape around her shoulders and swept out.

The mice in the room started buzzing about the coming rally and how they would try to convince all their friends and relatives to attend. Bridget was delighted that at last something was going to unite the mice in defying the terrible cats. They were about to leave to start rounding up mice to attend the rally when Fievel tapped Bridget on the shoulder and reminded her that they had come to speak to Honest John.

"Oh, I am sorry, Philly," said Bridget, and she went directly across the room to ask Honest John if he could help find Fievel's lost family.

"Their name is Mousekewitz," she explained to the politician.

"Happy to help, my dear. Have they registered to vote?" asked Honest John.

"I don't think so. They just got off the boat," replied Bridget.

"Nope, don't know 'em yet. Sorry, kid," Honest John said, and turned back to his cronies as Fievel sighed disappointedly. Another hope dashed to pieces.

Bridget put her arm around Fievel's shoulders. "Come on, Philly. Let's go home. You can stay at my place till you find your folks."

Late into the night, little Fievel sat looking out Bridget's window, staring at the moon, wondering where in the enormous darkened city his family might be.

At that same time, in another part of the city, his sister Tanya also sat at the window, looking at the moon, thinking about her lost brother Fievel. Papa sadly played Fievel's special tune on his violin. "I just know Fievel's alive," Tanya said, half to herself and half to the moon, hoping somehow Fievel would hear.

Chapter Seven
THE RALLY

The next day, thousands and thousands of mice turned out for the rally at Mausheimer Park. Mice of every nationality, every religion, every possible type and description showed up, all united by their fear and hatred of the cats.

"May I have your attention, please," shouted Gussie Mausheimer into a large megaphone. "I am very gratified by this outpouring. It is clear that we all feel something must be done about those horrible cats!"

Some of the mice in the audience became extremely nervous and called out, "Not so loud! The cats will hear you!" They glanced over their shoulders as if expecting to see the cats bearing down on them even as they spoke.

"Let them hear me," yelled Gussie. "These things must be said! We must have our freedom! Why did we all come here to America? For freedom!"

The crowd began to nod and murmur assent. "That's true."

"Look at that statue out there!" Gussie went on, pointing at the almost finished Statue of Liberty. "What does it stand for? *Freedom!*"

The mice nodded some more.

"So what is it that we want?" Gussie cried.

"Freedom!" they all yelled back to her.

"Right! Freedom from cats! And if we all work together, we can do it!"

"But they're bigger than we are!" yelled a mouse in the crowd.

"So?" said Gussie. "Are we men or are we mice?"

"We're mice!" they cried, cheering and throwing their hats into the air.

"So! What are we going to do about those cats?" Gussie yelled.

Suddenly there was total silence. Although their spirit was there, nobody had a single idea of how to stand up against the rampages of the cats. The mice shifted back and forth uncomfortably. Nobody could think of a thing.

Slowly, little Fievel held up his hand. "Um . . . I think I might have an idea," he said tentatively.

Fievel went up to the front of the platform and whispered his idea to Gussie Mausheimer. He recalled the "Giant Mouse of Minsk" story that his Papa had told him. He thought it would be useful now. Gussie went and whispered the idea to Honest John, who whispered it to the other mouse officials.

"Humph," said the police-chief mouse. "Fairy tales."

"Childish nonsense," complained the fire-chief mouse.

"What silliness," said Honest John.

"Just a moment," said Gussie. "I believe the little fellow just might have something."

Gussie went into a long huddle with the other officials and they whispered back and forth excitedly. Finally Gussie stepped back to the front of the platform and announced to the multitude, "This will take the cooperation of everybody, but I am pleased to announce that we have a plan!"

All the mice in the park cheered and cheered. Tony clapped Fievel on the back and Bridget gave him a big kiss. They couldn't wait to get started!

Over the next several days, the entire mouse community was a flurry of activity. Everybody had an assignment and everybody worked night and day. They picked a long winding street that began high on a hill and ran all the way down to a pier at the harbor. Some mice were responsible for building tall barricades out of rocks and boards and wooden boxes down the side of the street. Other mice carried hundreds of pebbles that they piled up in mounds near the top of the hill, where a huge wall would be constructed. Still other mice worked long into the night sewing pieces of cloth together into a giant quilt.

Everybody worked with energy and dedication. Gussie Mausheimer stood proudly on top of the barricades and shouted encouragement to the tireless workers.

"I'm proud of all of you," she cried. "Those cats will be sorry they ever messed with us!"

One day, as Fievel struggled to place a large stone on top of the barricade, he heard a plaintive sound. He stopped what he was doing and listened. Fievel caught his breath. It was the sound of a violin! He dropped the stone he was carrying and scampered down the wall.

"Papa?" he whispered.

Ears standing straight up, little Fievel started along the street, following the sound of the violin. He followed it around the corner, through an alley, and into a gutter. Slipping into a sewer to follow the sound of the music, Fievel found himself running through a long maze of dark underground tunnels, slippery and full of strange shadows and echoes. But the sound of the violin music pulled him along until he finally arrived at a door with a sign on it. The sign read:

MOTT STREET MAULERS/NO DOGS ALLOWED

It was the headquarters of the cats! Fievel peered through a window and saw four tough-looking cats sitting around a table, playing poker. One of the cats was complaining about the terrible violin playing. As Fievel scanned the room, his eyes widened with amazement. The violin player was none other than Warren T. Rat!

As Fievel stared, Warren T. Rat's arm banged into the end of his long rat nose.

"Rats!" complained Warren T. Rat. "This nose keeps getting in the way when I play!" Warren T. Rat strode to a mirror, grabbed his nose, and right before Fievel's astonished eyes, pulled it off. The rest of the rat face came off with the nose, revealing that Warren T. Rat was actually a cat in disguise!

As Warren admired himself in the mirror, he suddenly got a glimpse of little Fievel staring at him in amazement through the window.

"Uh, oh," said Warren, "the secret's out. Men, get me that mouse!"

All four of the poker-playing cats leapt out of their chairs and sped out the door after Fievel. It was a mad chase, back through the underground tunnels and up through the sewer grate. Fievel was just a few inches away from the safety of the barricades when a gigantic paw grabbed him from behind and pulled him back down into the sewer.

Chapter Eight
THE MOTT STREET MAULERS

Standing on top of the completed barricade wall, Gussie Mausheimer reviewed the plan once more with the leaders of the mouse forces. She pointed to a large boat that was docked at the pier at the end of the street.

"Don't forget," she said sternly, "the boat whistle blows at six o'clock in the morning. And that is when we must release our secret weapon. The cats must be here at exactly six—no sooner, no later! Is that clear?"

The mice all nodded enthusiastically.

"All right," said Gussie, "everybody get some sleep. We have a long day ahead!"

The mice all settled down to get whatever rest they could before the coming battle with the cats.

Meanwhile, down at the cats' headquarters, Fievel was locked up in a little cage and guarded by a particularly fierce-looking cat.

"My name is Tiger," snarled the guard. "Don't make any funny moves. I'm mean and I'm nasty and don't you forget it!"

Fievel looked out at Tiger's long white fangs and his sharp pointy claws. This was surely the end. He'd never see his family again. Never! He sat down on the floor of his cage and couldn't hold it in anymore. He started to sniffle, and before long he was sobbing as if his little heart would break.

"Aw, gee," said the cat, "don't do that. Was it something I said? What are you crying about, kid?"

"I lost my family and I've been looking all over for them," blubbered Fievel. "And now I'm locked up in here and I'll never get out and I'll never see them again!"

"You lost your family?" asked the cat. "Me too! I lost my whole family too! Eight brothers, ten sisters, three fathers . . ." And, amazingly, the ferocious cat started to cry as well.

"Gosh," said Fievel. "Maybe you could find them if you tried."

"You think so?" asked the cat. "Gee, that would be great. Do you like me? Y'know, I don't really have anything against mice. In fact, I think they're kinda cute. I don't even eat them. I'm a vegetarian, y'see. I like you."

"That's nice," said Fievel gloomily.

"C'mon now, cheer up," said Tiger. "You'll find your family."

"Not while I'm locked in here," said Fievel.

Tiger looked both ways. "You know what," he said to Fievel. "You're the first mouse that didn't hate me. I don't like those Maulers anyway, they're such bullies. Tell you what . . ." He took his keys and unlocked the door of Fievel's cage. "Now get going! Quick!"

As Tiger opened the door of the cage, an earsplitting alarm went off.

"Uh, oh," said Tiger. "I forgot about the alarm. Get outta here! Hurry!"

Fievel scampered out of the cage, gave Tiger a big hug of thanks, and dashed out the door. At that moment, hearing the alarm, Warren T. Rat and the other Mott Street Maulers came rushing into the room. They saw that the door of Fievel's cage was wide open and the cage was empty!

"After him! Quick!" Warren yelled to the cats who sped out the door after Fievel. "You—you—" Warren spluttered at Tiger. "You let him go! You're fired!"

"Aaah, I quit," said Tiger. "I never liked you guys anyway. I'm throwing my shirt in and splitting from this gang."

Fievel raced through tunnels and alleys, closely pursued by the furious cats. As he popped out of a piece of grating, he saw that he was very near the barricades and the hidden secret weapon of the mice.

Chapter Nine
THE GIANT MOUSE OF MINSK

On top of the wall, Gussie Mausheimer heard the scuffle of the cats chasing Fievel, and woke up the other mice.

"Oh, no!" she cried. "They're here too early! What are we gonna do? Wake up, everybody!"

Fievel raced to the barricades, took a flying leap, and landed on top of the parapet. A giant cat paw swiped across the top, just missing him by a hair.

"Keep them busy," shouted Gussie. "We must keep the cats here till the whistle blows at six!"

The mice danced around, taunting the cats and pelting them with rocks.

"Just a moment, hold your fire!" called Gussie. "Here comes that rat, Warren T. Rat!"

"He's not a rat," cried Fievel. "He's a cat! In disguise! That's a mask!"

"Pay no attention to that little mouse," said Warren T. Rat. "Listen to me. If you will throw down all your money and that little mouse, I think I can convince these cats to leave you alone."

The mice on the barricades looked over at Fievel and then back to Warren T. Rat.

"Don't listen to that faker!" yelled Tony, and picking up his slingshot, he flung a pebble right at Warren T. Rat. The pebble hit him in the face and knocked his fake rat nose right off!

"What's in a nose?" soothed Warren. "Doesn't mean a thing."

Tony shot another pebble and knocked Warren's rat ears off. The rest of his rat disguise hung in tatters around his head. It was clear that he was, indeed, a cat underneath!

"He *is* a cat!!" shouted the mice.

"C'mon," toyed Warren. "Who are you gonna believe, me or your own eyes?"

"Get him, men!" the mice all shouted.

"Oh, yeah?" leered Warren. "We'll see who's gonna get who!" He took out a large wooden match, struck it on his long teeth, and set fire to the bottom of the wall.

"Fire! Fire!" yelled the mice, racing around in a panic.

"Please! Stay calm!" yelled Gussie. "It's three minutes to six! It's almost time to release the secret weapon!"

The fire spread rapidly through the barricades. The cats watched gleefully, expecting the mice to jump off the walls into their outstretched paws.

Suddenly the boat in the harbor blew its whistle with an enormous reverberating blast.

"It's six o'clock!" cried Gussie. "At last! Release the secret weapon!"

Battalions of mice took their positions and started the procedure that would release the mysterious secret weapon. Dozens of mice pulled on heavy ropes, others pushed a lever that started a mammoth wheel rolling down the hill. There was a rumbling sound as the secret weapon started to roll toward the wall at the top of the hill.

The cats, hearing the rumbling sound, huddled in the middle of the street, wondering what was going on. Suddenly there was a tremendous crash and the secret weapon came hurtling through the wall, smashing it to smithereens and careening down the hill toward the cats. Fievel was hit by a piece of flying wood and knocked unconscious. He was thrown in one direction; his hat flew off in another.

"It's the Giant Mouse of Minsk!" screamed Warren T. Rat.

"I thought that was a fairy tale!" yelled another cat.

But this was no fairy tale. The mice had worked around the clock to build a gigantic mouse at least three stories tall. Its skin was a patchwork of thousands of pieces of cloth sewn into place by hundreds of mice. Its nose was a huge balloon and it had long, menacing teeth made of wood. The word MINSK was embroidered in huge letters across its chest. The mouse was mounted on a giant platform made of several pushcarts nailed together, and now this platform came rolling down the hill directly at the cats, going faster and faster.

"Yaggh!" screamed the cats, running through the barricades down the hill to escape the Giant Mouse of Minsk.

The barricades the mice had built led the cats directly to the dock. At the end of the dock, the boat that had blown its whistle was beginning to inch away from the pier. As the Giant Mouse of Minsk rolled nearer and nearer, the cats came to the end of the pier and, having nowhere else to go, leapt across the widening gap onto the fantail of the departing ship. Warren, the last cat of all,

jumped for the ship and missed, falling into the water. The other cats threw him a line and hauled him onto the boat, wet, cold, and fuming.

The Giant Mouse of Minsk rolled down the pier, too, and toppled off the end into the water, where it quickly sank.

The mice all lined up at the end of the pier and watched the boat steam away. The cats on board shook their fists angrily.

"Look," cried Tony. "Look at the name of that boat. It's the *Ocean Princess Hong Kong!!* Those cats are going to Hong Kong!"

The mice all cheered.

On the boat, Warren turned to his cohorts. "Don't worry fellas," he said. "I'm sure there are plenty of mice in Hong Kong."

"Phooey," responded the other cats.

Back at the barricades, both mice and human firefighters were working hard to put out the fire the cats had set. Tony and Bridget ran through the confusion trying to find Fievel.

"Philly! Philly Mousekewitz!" they called.

Fievel, lying unconscious on the sidewalk, had been picked up by a stream of water from the firehose. The water swept him along the gutter and finally deposited him in a wet pile of straw in an alley.

"Tony, look," cried Bridget. "That's Philly's hat!" They picked up the hat and renewed the search for their little friend. "He must be around here somewhere. Philly! Philly Mousekewitz!"

Just at that moment, Mama and Papa Mousekewitz came running by with Tanya and Yasha.

"Listen," said Tanya. "Those mice are calling for a Philly Mousekewitz! I got this feeling it's Fievel!"

"How could it be Fievel?" asked Mama. "Philly isn't Fievel. If they were looking for Fievel, they'd be calling *Fievel!*"

"C'mon Papa. I wanna find out," said Tanya.

"Look, I would love nothing more than to find our Fievel, but we can't keep clinging to false hope. Once and for all, I'll show you that Fievel is gone forever," said Papa. He marched over to Tony and Bridget. "Excuse me," he said. "You are calling for someone named Philly Mousekewitz. Would you please tell my daughter that the mouse you are looking for is named Philly, and not Fievel?"

"Well," said Tony, "his name is Philly . . . and *also* Fievel."

"Fievel, Shmievel," said Papa. "There could be a thousand Fievel Mousekewitzes in New York. Doesn't mean it's *our* Fievel Mousekewitz."

But Mama yelled, "Look! That's his hat!"

Tony held up Fievel's hat. Papa clutched the hat and gave it a big kiss. "That *is* his hat! Fievel!" he cried. "My son! He's alive!" Papa's heart nearly burst with joy.

"You are the Mousekewitzes!" said Bridget. "Philly's been looking

everywhere for you!"

"Oh, my! Oh, my! Oh, my!" said Papa, dancing. "My boy is alive! Alive! Alive! Where is he?"

"That's just it," said Tony. "We can't find him. He's lost."

"That's why we were calling him," explained Bridget. "We've been looking for him all day."

"Well, let's *all* look for him," cried Tanya. "What are we waiting for!"

The mice all started racing around calling "Fievel" or "Philly" as loud as they could. Up in a high tree, munching on a stalk of celery, their cries were heard by the big cat, Tiger, the one who had helped Fievel to escape from the Mott Street Maulers.

"Hmm," Tiger murmured to himself. "They're trying to find my little mouse friend. Perhaps I could help them. Now let me see . . . how do I get down from here . . . hmm. . . ."

Chapter Ten
REUNION

Meanwhile, in the alley, Fievel woke up and shook himself off. When he looked around, he saw there were several other mice in the alley, all living in dilapidated shacks made of cardboard and straw.

"Hey, there's a new kid on the block," said one mouse, noticing Fievel. "What're you doin' here, huh?"

"I've been looking for my family," sighed Fievel, sitting down on a battered tin can.

"He's lookin' for his family!" laughed the mouse. "Can you beat that! We gave up lookin' for our families ages ago!"

"Yeah, you'll never find 'em," said another mouse. "In a city this size with this many mice, forget it. They never found you and you'll never find them! You may as well stay here with us in Orphan Alley."

"I guess you're right," said Fievel sadly. "I guess this will be my home from now on."

Fievel pushed some straw together and made himself a rough bed next to the wall. As he lay down on it, he kept saying to himself, "I'll never see them again . . . never . . . never . . ."

Almost as if in a dream, Fievel heard the strains of violin music. He figured that he was imagining, remembering the old days in Russia when his Papa would play the violin for him . . . and he murmured again, "Never . . . never . . . never . . ."

Suddenly he sat up in his straw bed.

"Hey," he said. "Do you guys hear a violin?"

"Sure, kid," said one of the other mice. "So what. Lots of mice play the violin in this city."

"Yeah," said Fievel, "but only *one* mouse knows *that* song! That's my special song!"

Jumping up, Fievel raced out of the alley to the street.

Fievel tore through the streets, trying to pick up the strains of the special song! "Papa! *Papa!*" he called.

Way down at the far end of the street, Fievel spied a most peculiar procession. Tiger the cat came striding along with Papa, Mama, Tanya, Yasha, Gussie, Tony, and Bridget riding on his back. Papa stood up, playing Fievel's special song as loudly as he could.

"*Papa!*" yelled Fievel. "*Papa, it's me!*"

Everything stopped. Papa and Mama slid off the cat's back and ran to the middle of the street. Fievel ran to them from the other end of the street and they clutched each other and cried. Tony and Bridget hugged each other and danced

around with joy. Tanya jumped up and down. Gussie found herself hugging Tiger's leg with happiness.

Tanya gave Fievel a big hug. "I knew you were all right," she said. "I knew it all along."

"Mama! Papa! Tanya! Little Yasha!" Fievel couldn't get enough kisses and hugs.

"My little boy—back from the dead," sobbed Mama. "America! What a place!"

"Fievel, my little Fievel! I thought I'd never see you again, cried Papa, overwhelmed with happiness.

"Never say never, Papa," said Fievel.

"Here, Papa," said Tanya. "Here's Fievel's hat."

Papa took the hat and placed it back on Fievel's head.

"Ha, *ha!* Look!" exclaimed Papa. "It is starting to fit!"

Epilogue
AMERICA 1886

One day, several weeks later, Fievel had a special visitor. It was Henri the Pigeon.

"Do you remember me? I told you I would come to get you when my statue was finished!" he announced. "I want you to see her! She is so beautiful!"

"I found my family. Can I bring them with me?" asked Fievel.

"But of course," said Henri, smiling. "I want everyone to see her! Come, let us go."

Fievel and Tanya rode on Henri's back. Another pigeon carried Mama and Papa and Yasha, and a third pigeon arrived to carry Tony and Bridget.

They soared high above New York City and circled around the magnificent statue that now stood proudly in the harbor.

"Oh, she's wonderful," breathed Fievel.

"*Merci*," said Henri. "I am glad you like her."

"Henri," asked Fievel, pointing to the horizon far to the west. "What's that out there?"

"That is the rest of America!" said Henri.

"Wow!" said Fievel. "I'd like to see *that* someday."

"You will, my little immigrant," said the pigeon with a smile as he soared up into the clear blue sky. "You will!"

63